DIARY

OF A

MINECRAFT ZOMBIE

Book 7

Zack Zombie

Monday

"We're going where?!!"

"We're going to our Zombie family reunion," my Mom said.

Oh man, this is terrible! I thought I was going to spend the rest of my summer just playing video games and eating cake. Now I have to go to a dumb family reunion.

"Do I have to go, Mom?"

"Yes, you do. Our family reunion only comes around once every 100 years, and this year all of your relatives from all of the different Biomes are going to be there," she said.

Oh, great. I thought my family was crazy enough. Now I have to deal with the rest

of my crazy family from all around the Overworld.

I'm telling you I think somebody somewhere put a curse on me.

I mean this stuff doesn't happen to other 12 year old kids, does it?

I bet you human kids don't have to go to family reunions. I'm sure they don't have to deal with all of their crazy relatives coming together to do dumb family stuff.

Human kids probably have fun summers, just playing video games all day and eating lots of cake.

Man, being a Zombie is hard.

"Where is it going to be?" I asked my Mom.

"This year we're going to have it at the Grand Zombie Canyon in the Mesa Biome," she said.

"What's that?"

"Well, the Grand Zombie Canyon was where the last battle of the Zombie Apocalypse was fought," she said. "It has a lot of history, you know."

All of a sudden, Dad chimed in, "Yeah, your great, great, great, great grandpa Rhemus fought in that battle, and he said it was a real doozy."

That sounded pretty interesting...

"Really, Dad?"

"Yeah, Rhemus was a 37 star General in the Zombie Special Forces," Dad said. "He hobbled around really slow because of all those medals."

Whoa.

"And guess what, your great, great, great, great grandpa Rhemus is coming to the family reunion this year," Dad said with pride in his voice. "You can meet him."

"Your great, great, great grandmother Petunia Zombie flew across the ocean in a single engine airplane," Mom said, nodding. "She's coming too."

"Really?"

"And you know who else is coming?" Dad asked. "Your great, great, great, great, great, great grandpa Methuselah Zombie is coming. We're going to celebrate his 1000th birthday at the family reunion."

"What? He's going to be 1000 years old?!!"

"Yep." Dad nodded. "And he's just as rotten and smelly as when he first became a Zombie."

Wow. I never thought my family was that interesting. But great, great, great, great grandpa Rhemus and Petunia Zombie, and Methuselah Zombie all sound really cool.

I wonder what other cool relatives I'm going to meet at my Zombie family reunion.

Tuesday

I went to see Steve today to tell him about my Zombie family reunion.

I told him all about my cool relatives.

"And I have a great, great, great, great, great, great grandfather named Methuselah Zombie, whose going to turn 1000 years old."

"Wow! That's a long time to be a Zombie," Steve said.

"Yeah, I know, right?"

"Hey, Zombie, since you brought that up, I have a question for you."

"What is it?"

"Do Zombies ever die? I mean, I know you're already dead and stuff, but do you ever die, die?" Steve asked.

"I don't think so." I shook my head as I thought about it. "I asked my Dad once, and he said that as long as nothing major happens to us, like getting a serious blow to the head, Zombies can live forever."

"Whoa," Steve said. "But, if Zombies never die, wouldn't you run out of places to live?"

"My Dad said that there are plenty of caves for all the Zombies in the Overworld. He also said that the Overworld never ends. It just keeps generating more caves and biomes and stuff."

"Cool," Steve said.

"So, Steve, how would you feel about coming to my Zombie family reunion?" I asked him.

"Are you serious? That would be awesome. But won't your relatives get weirded out by me being human and all?"

"I think with a little green paint, and a little bit of old rotten Chinese food, we can fix all that," I said. "We can just tell them that you're an exchange student from another Biome. We get those all the time. They won't be able to tell the difference."

"Sweet. So when is it?"

"We're leaving on Sunday," I said.

"Wow, Zombie. Your family reunion is going to be off the hook!" Steve said.

"Yeah, I can't wait," I said, thinking it'd be even better with Steve there.

Wednesday

Today my Mom and Dad were talking about our Zombie family reunion.

"Dad, how are we going to get to the Zombie Family Reunion?"

"Well, son, the best way is by Minecart train."

"Minecart train? What's that?"

"Well, minecart trains are cars that travel on a powered rail," he said. "They're really a lot of fun when you travel across the Biomes."

"How long is it going to take?"

"It's going to take a few days to get there," he said. "That's why we're going to take the new sleeper Minecart trains. We get to sleep in them too."

"Really? Do they have beds in them?"

"They're more like body bags actually… Bunk bed style," he said.

Whoa, bunk body bags! That sounds so cool. Except I hope Mom and Dad don't put me with my little brother. He's such a pain, I thought.

"And don't worry, Zombie, you won't have to share a bunk body bag with your little brother," Mom said with a knowing look.

Whoa, did she just read my mind?

"Because your cousin Piggy is coming with us," Mom added. "His parents have a conference to go to in the Nether Fortress, so they'll be joining us at the reunion later. They're dropping Piggy off with us because they want him to get to the reunion early."

I didn't know how I felt about that. I mean, I like Piggy and all, but he can be a bit of a pain sometimes. He's kind of awkward too. And he always smells like bacon.

"You can share a bunk body bag with Piggy," Mom said.

Great, my trip will be full of dreams of Zombie bacon, I thought.

This was my chance to see if I could get them to bring Steve on the trip.

"Hey Mom, there's a Summer Exchange Student program at my school, and err… I was thinking that we can invite an exchange student to come be part of our Zombie family reunion."

"That is so nice of you, Zombie!" My Mom beamed. "Honey, did you hear that? Our baby is thinking of how to help others. I think I'm going to cry…"

Then my Mom let out the waterworks. It was working like a charm.

"Son, I'm real proud of you for thinking of the needs of others," Dad said. "We would be happy to host an exchange student."

Ha! It worked.

"Oh, OK. I'll tell Ms. Bones at summer school and she'll take care of it," I said.

This is so cool. Now Steve can come on our Zombie family reunion!

Only thing is... Steve kinda smells funny too.

Thursday

Today I was really missing my friends Skelee, Slimey and Creepy.

I really missed my ghoulfriend Sally too.

They were all doing something different with their families for the summer so they weren't around.

Skelee was spending the summer at Yellowbone National Park where his family was from.

Slimey was still at the Superflat Biome with his family. Slimey really liked the open fields where he could jump around and have fun and stuff. So he's having a good time out there.

14

After Creepaway Camp, Creepy went to visit his cousin Archie in the Nether. Except, I still don't know why all that heat in the Nether doesn't bother him.

And Sally was still on her world tour of all the Biomes. She wasn't coming back until a few days before school.

I really miss Sally, too. I liked going to the Zombie's Café and sharing a nice snot shake with her.

I know what I'll do, I thought. *I'll go see Mutant.*

So I went to visit Mutant at his house next to the Nuclear Waste factory.

When I got there, Mutant was outside playing with all of his rabbit friends.

The weird thing about Mutant's rabbit friends is that they're all a bit deformed. Some of them have three eyes. Some have six legs. And a few of them have more than one head.

But those are the normal ones. The deformed ones have only two eyes and four legs.

"Hey Mutant!"

16

UUURRRRGGHHH!!!

"Whatcha up to?"

UUURRRRGGHHH!!!

"Just playing with your rabbit friends?"

UUURRRRGGHHH!!!

"And one of them just had babies?"

UUURRRRGGHHH!!!

"And you named one of them Zombie?"

UUURRRRGGHHH!!!

"Wow, thanks buddy. That was real nice of you."

Then I told him, "Guess what? I'm going to a Zombie family reunion in a few days."

UUURRRRGGHHH!!!

"Yeah, I know it's really awesome."

17

UUURRRRGGHHH!!!

"No, my friends couldn't come. They're out doing different things this summer. But I wish they were coming… By the way, what are you doing for the rest of the summer?"

UUURRRRGGHHH!!!

"You're going to go visit your relatives in the desert? Wow, I didn't know you had any relatives."

UUURRRRGGHHH!!!

"Yeah, my relatives are weird too."

You know, I really like talking to Mutant. He's a great listener.

I don't actually understand what he's saying most of the time, but I think we still understand each other.

We have a real special connection.

Friday

Ding DONG!

"Zombie, can you get the door? I think that's your cousin Piggy."

So I went to the door, and it was Piggy and his Dad.

Except Piggy looked a little different. I think Dad said that puberty does weird things to kids. I guess puberty must be hard on Zombie Pigmen.

"Hey Piggy," I said.

"Hey Zombie, check out my new gold sword," he said. "My Mom and Dad just got it for me for my birthday."

"Yeah son, I think you're growing into a fine young Zombie Pigman," Piggy's Dad said.

"It's about time you had your own sword to battle those evil brain eating humans, he, he."

"Take that, and take that, you evil humans!" Piggy said as he wildly waved his sword around.

"Hey, watch the sword, killer," I said. "We're short on extra Zombie parts right now."

"Hey there Francis," Zombie's Dad said to my Dad.

"Hey Lionel," Dad said.

"Thanks for taking Piggy with you to the Zombie family reunion," Piggy's Dad said. "I was trying to get out of the Nether Fortress Conference, but when the Ghasts, Wither Skeletons, Blazes and the Zombie Pigmen Committee gets together, things can get really heated. So I need to be there to calm things down."

I think Piggy's Dad is somebody important in the Nether. He's some kind of ambassador or something. I think that's probably why they live so close to the Nether Fortress. Only problem is, the Nether Fortress is in the middle of the Nether so it's really, really hot. It can be a problem for regular Zombies. We don't sweat, you know.

"Not a problem, Lionel. We'll take good care of him," My Dad assured him.

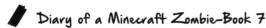

"Hey Piggy, go check out your room, it's the second one on the left upstairs," Dad said.

"Thanks, Mr. Zombie," Piggy said as he ran up the stairs waving his new gold sword.

Wait a minute, I thought. *My room is the second one on the left.*

"Good bye, Lionel. We'll see you at the reunion."

I think my Dad waited for Piggy's Dad to leave so he could drop the bomb on me.

"Piggy's going to be staying in your room until we leave," Dad said. "It's that OK with you?"

All I know is that Mom wasn't the only one that could turn on the waterworks.

"Blahhhhhhhhh!!!!!" I cried.

I think Dad wasn't ready for that.

"It's only for few days," he said.

But all I heard was, "And Piggy is going to break all your toys, he's going to rip up all of your comics, and he's going to eat your booger collection."

"Blahhhhhhhhh!!!!!"

My life is officially over, I thought, as I cried myself to sleep on the living room couch.

Saturday

Today, I had to get Steve ready so I could introduce him to my parents.

We got some green Zombie lady makeup from the mobware store to help him look more Zombie-like.

I don't know why Zombie ladies wear makeup. It makes them look really weird. I'm not used to seeing a Zombie with smooth green skin.

Anyway, we put on as much as we could so that he was totally covered from head to toe.

After we finished, Steve looked awesome.

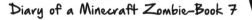

So we went to my house to meet my Mom and Dad.

My Mom answered the door.

"Hi Zombie. And who is this young Zombie?"

"Ello, Mrs. Zombie, My nem is Zven from Zveden," Steve said in his best Zvedish accent.

"Hello, Zven. It's great to have you in our home," Mom said.

"Ya, I am very habby to be heer!"

Actually, I think Steve was pouring it on really thick. I thought Mom would see through his act for sure.

"Errr, Mom, I want to show Zven my room." I grabbed him by the arm to get him out of there.

"That's a good idea, Zombie. I'll prepare some pillows for him and he can sleep with you in the living room," Mom said.

After Mom left, Steve and I couldn't hold it in any more.

"PPFFTTTTTT!!!!!" We burst out laughing.

"Zven from Zveden? Where'd you get that from? Couldn't you be like 'Larry' from the

Forrest Biome or 'Emery' from the Swamp
Biome or something?" I said laughing.

"I couldn't help it," Steve said, "it just came
to me."

"Well, I hope you don't mind the smell of
bacon," I told Steve as we entered the room.

When we walked in, Piggy was there reading
my comics.

"Hey Zombie," Piggy said. "Who's your
friend?"

Before I could answer, Piggy rushed on. "Hi,
friend of Zombie's, my name is Piggy. I'm a
Zombie Pigman, and I have a gold sword. I
use it to kill brain eating humans!" Then he
started waving his sword around and almost
gave me and Steve matching haircuts.

"Piggy, put your sword away," I told him. "I
told you we have a shortage of extra Zombie

body parts in the house because Dad didn't go to the Morgue this week."

I actually lied. We had plenty of extra Zombie parts. Except lips. For some reason, we haven't had those in years.

Then my Mom called me downstairs for something.

"Zombie!" Mom yelled.

"Hey Mom," I said as I walked downstairs.

"How's Zven doing?" Mom asked. "Is he getting settled in?"

"He's great. Zven and Piggy really hit it off. They're in my room playing with my booger collection right now."

"OK… well, we're having dinner soon, so please tell Piggy and Zven to get ready," she said.

"Oh, Ok. I will Mom."

"Oh, and can you tell Zven to freshen up a little bit… He smells kind of funny."

Sunday

We went to the minecart train station today to leave for our reunion, and I got to see a minecart train for the first time.

It was really cool.

It looked like about one hundred minecarts that were linked together.

There were a lot of mob families that got on the minecart train. I saw a lot of Zombies, some Creepers, and Skeletons, and I even saw a Slime family try to get on.

Though I think they had trouble squeezing in the small doorway.

Dad told me that most minecart trains aren't covered, but we needed a roof so we wouldn't get burned by the sun on our long trip. We were going across the country, so it would take a few days.

Dad also told me that when they built the first cross country minecart trains, nobody thought about adding a cover. It was one of the worst disasters in mob history.

Dad says that mobs aren't all that smart.

I was looking at all of the minecarts and wondering how they all stuck together.

"Hey Dad," I asked him, "What keeps all of the minecarts together?"

"That's a good question, son," he said. "They're usually joined by a pin that connects the cars together. You know, one time, a kid accidentally pulled one of the pins, and when the train left the station, some of the cars were left behind."

"Whoa."

So we boarded the minecart train and went to the back two cars.

Steve, Piggy, my little brother Wesley and I were all in the last car, and Mom and Dad were in the car next to us.

It was already late, so we all got into our bunk bed body bags.

Steve was a little taller than the rest of us, so we had to cut a hole in the bottom of his body bag so he could fit. His feet were sticking out of the bottom and dangling over his bunk.

His feet were kind of smelly too, so the minecart train car smelled like pickles and pig's feet.

I'm so looking forward to getting to our Zombie family reunion. I never knew that we had so many cool mobs in my family.

Well, we get there tomorrow, so I'm going to sleep.

This is turning out to be the best summer ever...

Special Sunday Entry

Thud!

We all woke up because it felt like we ran into something.

I looked out the window and it was a little after sundown. All the other guys had woken up too.

Then I saw everybody getting off the train, so we got off the train too.

"What is it?" I asked my Dad.

"Oh, it's OK, son. We just made a stop in the desert before we make it to the Mesa Biome," Dad said. "People are getting a little stretch and a bit of fresh desert air."

I could sure use some fresh desert air after being in the minecart with Steve and Piggy.

There's only so much pickles and bacon I can take.

So everybody in the minecart train got out and just wandered about for a while.

When it was time to leave, I noticed that my little brother Wesley was missing, so I went looking for him.

When I found him, he was waving a gold stick that looked like Piggy's sword.

"Shiny!" Wesley said.

"Wesley, don't play with Piggy's sword," I said. "He's not going to like it."

Plus I'm not sure we brought any extra body parts… What if Wesley cut off his hand or something? And I'd probably get blamed for it.

35

So I picked up Wesley and Piggy's sword, and we got on the Minecart train right when it was about to leave.

I put Wesley in his body bag bunk and I thought, *Wesley is such a pest! Why do Mom and Dad have to bring him everywhere?*

So then I jumped into my body bag and decided to get some more sleep.

I really hate waking up early…

Monday Early Entry

*Y*AWN!

Man it felt great to get some sleep.

The train wasn't moving so I thought we probably arrived.

I wonder why Mom and Dad didn't wake us up?

Well, I was just glad to be here.

"Wake up, fellas, we're here!" I said.

"Whuzzat?" Steve said.

"Ruyeek, ruyeek, ruyeeek" Piggy said while swinging his sword.

I think I woke Piggy up from a bad dream.

"You OK, Piggy?"

"I just had the weirdest dream that we were attacked by brain eating humans, with giant pumpkin heads!" he said.

"Don't worry, it was just a dream."

Then I noticed that Wesley was sleeping with Piggy's sword. But Piggy had his sword in his hand.

If Piggy has his sword in his hand, then what was Wesley holding?

Oh, no...

So I jumped out of the bunk bed and ran outside.

We were still in the desert, and the rest of the train was gone!

Wesley had pulled the pin that held the train cars together!

I thought, *UUUURRRGGGHHHH!!!! LITTLE BROTHERS ARE SUCH A PEST! I WISH WESLEY HAD NEVER BEEN BORN!*

Then Steve, Piggy and my little brother came out of the car and watched me jump up and down.

"Whoa, you OK there, Zombie?" Steve asked.

Piggy thought I was attacking imaginary brain eating humans so he started jumping along with me and swinging his gold sword.

Wesley got into it too, and started swinging the gold minecart pin like a sword.

UUURRRGGGHHHH!!!

"So where's the rest of the train?" Piggy asked.

It took me a while to calm down so I could explain what happened.

"Wesley pulled the minecart pin, so the rest of the minecart train left without us," I said. "We're stuck here!"

"Shiny," Wesley said as he kept jumping around and waving the minecart pin in my face.

UUURRRGGGHHHH!!!

"Calm down there, buddy," Steve said. "I guess we'll just have to figure out a way to get there. But right now we have bigger problems."

Steve pointed to the horizon, and the sun was rising. We had slept straight till daybreak. So, we had to get into a cave quick.

We saw a big rock cliff far away, so we ran for it.

Steve put Wesley on his shoulders, because I was too mad at him to help him. We picked up anything we could carry and ran as fast as we could.

"Shiny, shiny, shiny, shiny…"was all we heard as we ran toward the hills.

All of a sudden, I smelled that bacon smell again, except this time I heard sizzling too.

Piggy had fallen behind because he was a slow runner. So I ran back to get him.

I gave him a piggyback ride all the way to the hills.

"Can't you throw that sword away?" I told Piggy. "It's making you really heavy."

"We may need it to fight off brain eating humans," he said.

UUURRRGGGHHHH!!!

We made it to the hills and saw a cave in front of us.

We made it into the cave just in time, as the sun came out full blast.

"Shiny!" Wesley said pointing to the sunrise.

We were stuck in that cave for a long time.

After a while we got really tired. So we all decided to get some sleep.

So we all fell asleep to the smell of crispy bacon.

Monday Entry

"**H**ey Zombie, I think somebody's outside," Steve said as he woke me up.

"Uurrghwhuzzwhat?"

"Crackle!"

Then I heard it too.

It was dark out, so we could go out of the cave, but none of us wanted to.

It was the first time I saw Steve scared of anything, so I knew we were in trouble.

"What do you think it is?" I asked Steve.

"I don't know. But the people in my village have been telling stories lately, about wild green creatures in the desert that sneak up on you and blow you up if you're not looking," he said.

"Whoa," I said.

"Crackle!"

"It's coming closer!" I said.

"We're gonna have to get ready for battle." Steve picked up a rock.

"Piggy, are you ready to fight some brain eating humans?" Steve said to Piggy.

"Ready for duty, Sir!" Piggy gave a salute.

"How about you, little bro," Steve said to Wesley. "Are you ready for battle?"

"Shiny," Wesley said, holding up the minecart pin.

So me and Steve looked at each other and gave each other a nod.

Then we rushed out all at once, yelling,
"AAAAAHHHHH!!!!"

But nobody was outside.

Steve and I looked at each other and started
giggling and laughing. Then all of us started
laughing.

All of a sudden, all of these monsters jumped
out from the bushes around us.

"UUURRRGGHHH!!!"

"AAAAHHHHHHH!" we said as we cowered
together into a ball.

Then one of the monsters reached out its claw
to sink into us and I just closed my eyes.

"Piggy, izzat you?" The beast said. "Whatcha
dering so far from home?"

"Uncle Rufus?" Piggy said surprised.
"Zombie, it's uncle Rufus, my Dad's second

45

uncle's son's, cousin's brother, twice removed."

"Hey everyberdy, it's Lionel's son Piggy!" Rufus said, with a weird accent I could hardly understand.

"Heerrraayyyy!!!" the group yelled as more Zombies came out of the bushes.

"Watcha doing out here by yer lonesome?" Rufus asked.

"We were on our way to the Zombie family reunion and our minecart got separated from the others," I said.

Rufus looked me over and then smiled, "You must be Francis' son, Zombie!"

"Hey everyberdy, it's Francis's son Zombie!"

"Heerrraayyyy!!!" they all yelled.

46

Hey, I didn't mind the introductions, but what I really wanted to know was how to get to the Mesa Biome.

"And hurz this little guy?" Rufus asked looking at Wesley.

"That's my little brother, Wesley, but what we want to know is how to get to the Mesa…"

"Hey everyberdy, it's Francis's son Wesley!"

"Heerrraayyyy!!!" they all yelled.

"And hurz this smelly young Zombie?" Rufus asked pointing to Steve.

"That's my friend Ste…uh Zven from Zveden, but how do we get to the…"

"Hey everyberdy, it's Zombie's friend Zven from Zveden!"

"Heerrraayyyy!!!" they all yelled.

Man we were getting nowhere with these guys.

Uncle Rufus started introducing all of our relatives to us, but there were like a thousand of them so I knew we were going to be there for a few hours.

"And this is Zeke, and Billy-Bob, and Billy-Ray, and Mabel, and Cletus, and Clyde, and Eustuce, and Floyd and Otis, and Roscoe, and Betty-Lou and…"

I couldn't take it anymore!

"CAN ANYBODY TELL US HOW TO GET TO THE MESA BIOME?!!!" I yelled. "WE NEED TO GET TO OUR ZOMBIE FAMILY REUNION!!!"

Then everybody got quiet.

"Why didn't yer say yer going to the Zombie family reunion?" Rufus said smiling.

"Hey everyberdy, they're going to the Zombie family reunion!"

"Heerrraayyyy!!!" they all said.

"It's a night's walk in that direction," Uncle Rufus said pointing to the desert. "We would walk yer, but it's mining season, and we need to go scare some miners silly, right boys?!!"

"Heerrraayyyy!!!" they all yelled.

"Thank you, Uncle Rufus," I said, glad to get out of there.

"We'll join yer at the family reunion in a few days after we scare some miners!" Rufus said as we walked away. "Right boys?!!!"

"Heerrraayyyy!!!" they all yelled.

Monday Night Entry

After leaving Uncle Rufus and our Zillbilly family, we started walking toward the Mesa Biome.

We walked for hours, and it was really hot and really scary.

We were all still scared after Steve told us about the strange green creatures that blow people up.

At first, I thought he was talking about Creepers. But Creepers only blow up by accident.

Actually, I'm really surprised my friend Creepy back home hasn't blown up yet. He's kind of clumsy sometimes.

But I think Creepy said that they've made so many advances in science that by using a liquid Nitrogen inhaler, a Creeper can go explosion free for a long time.

Well, I'm just glad Creepy is not here, I thought. *Knowing him he would probably forget his inhaler. And Creepers and desert cactus don't mix very well.*

I was lost in my thoughts until Steve took out his harmonica and broke out into a song:

"Home, Home on the raaaange…

Where the spiders and silverfish plaaaay.

Where seldom is seeeeen,

An exploding-monster that's greeeeen,

And the sun…oops, sorry…and the mooooon glows brightly all day!"

51

We all laughed at Steve's singing, but I think Piggy was still scared. He was holding onto his gold sword really tight.

Then we heard, BOOM!

We turned around and looked to the left and looked to right to see where it came from.

Piggy was swinging his sword wildly in every direction with his eyes closed. "Take that, and that, and that, and that!"

"Piggy!" I said. "Whatever it was, I think it's gone now."

"I think you spoke too soon," Steve said pointing. "Look!"

We saw a shadow of the weirdest creature far away, but it looked like it was coming toward us.

"Oh man, oh man, oh man, oh man, oh man, oh man," Piggy said.

Then it crept out of the shadows and it was…
a Creeper! But a weird looking Creeper. It
looked like it had been out here for a long
time.

Weirdest thing was that it had a Hawaiian
shirt on.

"What arrrr you guysssss doing heeere?" the
Creeper said, slurring his words really slowly.
"Are yoooo trying to get my berrrrrieesss?

"Berries?" I said, "No we're just trying to get
to the Mesa Biome."

"Oh, thasss gooood because I would
prooooobably have to get tough with
yooooou guyssss, if you were." The Creeper
could barely stand up.

Steve bent down to look at the plants next to
him with berries on them. "You mean these
berries?"

"Yeah, thoooose are my berrrrriiiiesss, so don't tusssh them, OK?"

Then Steve whispered to me, "Hey Zombie, these are Ender Berries. You eat enough of these, they make you really loopy."

"How long have you've been eating these?" Steve asked the Creeper.

"We've been eatttttting theeezzz for the past few munths, since our tour bussss got losssst out heeeere," he said.

"Where are the rest of the Creepers from the tour bus?"

BOOOOMMM!

"Theressss one of them now," the Creeper said.

54

All of a sudden, we knew we were in trouble. The Creeper was standing right next to a cactus, and by the look of things, he was about to fall over.

Steve picked up my little brother Wesley, and yelled, "RUN!!!"

Piggy and I jumped into the bushes and then…

BOOOOOOMM!

"Is everybody OK?" Steve said.

"Yeah, we're good. But look at that!" I looked down at the big crater the Creeper made.

The Creeper's explosion made an opening in the ground that revealed an underground tunnel.

"Whoa, that must be an underground mineshaft or something," Steve said.

Then Wesley said, "Shiny," as he pointed to the horizon.

"Oh man, the sun's rising," I said. "Let's jump into the mineshaft quick."

So all of us jumped into the mineshaft to keep from getting burned.

It was really dark in there.

But none of us cared, because we were all really tired from walking.

Piggy, Wesley and Steve flopped on the ground and fell asleep.

I stayed up a bit just thinking.

Are we ever going to get to my Zombie family reunion? I thought. *Or are we going to be stuck out here forever?*

I really hope we make it. I really want to meet Grandpa Methuselah.

His birthday cake must be huge…

Tuesday

I woke up to a really bright light.

"Wake up, Zombie," Steve said. "I found something."

"Uuurggghhhyyyaawwwnn! What time is it?"

"I don't know," Steve said. "But check this out."

Steve had a torch that he brought with him, and he held it up against the wall.

On the wall were all of kinds of Egyptian Zombie pictures.

"Whoa," Piggy said. "I know what those are. Those are Egyptian Zombie hieroglyphics."

"Hiro-what?"

"Hieroglyphics," Piggy said. "They're ancient Egyptian Zombie writing. There's a museum of Mob Natural History in the Nether Fortress that my Mom takes me to sometimes. They have a whole exhibit with a bunch of these on the walls. My Mom even got me a book on how to translate them."

"Do you think you can read these?" Steve asked.

"Maybe… Let's see. Here lies the river…no, no… Here lies the path…right! Here lies the path to the ancient Egyptian Zombie treasure. Be wary…no… Beware… Beware all who enter here. Only the most noble will survive."

"Really? That's what it says? It doesn't say 'here is the fluffy minecart that will take you safely to your Zombie family reunion?'" I said, annoyed at another deathtrap.

"Nope, that's what it says," Piggy said.

"Where's your spirit of adventure?" Steve asked me.

"I left it on the minecart train with Mom and Dad," I said sarcastically.

"Well, that's the direction toward the Mesa Biome," Steve said pointing down the dark tunnel. "So we might as well see if we can find some Egyptian Zombie treasure along the way."

Oh, man, we're dead, I thought.

So, as we walked down the tunnel, Piggy kept talking.

"You know, Mummies were some of the original Zombies thousands of years ago," Piggy said. "They were really smart. They were great engineers and scientists."

"If they were so smart, why did they look so dumb?" I said, make-believing that I was an Egyptian Zombie. "Look at me, I'm an Egyptian Dummy."

"That's Mummy," Piggy said.

Steve started laughing. "Hey Piggy, what did the Egyptian Zombie engineers and scientists specialize in, anyway?"

"Booby traps," Piggy said.

Steve and I stopped dead in our tracks and looked at each other.

"Shiny!" Wesley said.

We turned his way, yelling, "NO!"

It was too late. He pulled a gold lever on the wall.

Suddenly, the entire floor caved in and we all fell through it.

"AAAAAAAHHHHH!!!!"

THUD! THUD! THUD!

We all landed in a strange room lit with torches.

"Cough, cough… Where's Wesley?" Steve asked.

THUD! Then Wesley landed right on top of me.

"Zumbie," Wesley said smiling.

UUUUURRGGHH!!!! Wesley makes me so mad!!!!!!

"Wesley, don't touch anything!" I yelled.

Then Wesley turned from green to blue, to red and… "WAAAAHHHH!!!!" Wesley started crying.

"Zombie, he's just a little kid, you know," Steve said. "Give him a break."

How is it that Wesley causes all the trouble, and I'm the bad guy! UUUURRGGHH!!!! I wish I never had a little brother!

Steve put Wesley on his shoulders. "Let's just find a way out of here. Where are we anyway?"

"I know where we are," Piggy said. "The orange and blue tiles and the large pillars

63

means... We must be in the main chamber of the desert temple!"

"Really? I've heard of the desert temple," Steve said. "Isn't there supposed to be a really big treasure in here?"

"Yes. But it's also supposed to be booby trapped," Piggy said. "If you step on the wrong floor block, the entire room will explode."

All of us looked at each other, and we froze in place.

"So what do we do?" I asked Piggy.

"I don't know," he said shrugging his shoulders.

"I got an idea," Steve said. "Let's dig through the blocks we're standing on now. They're not booby trapped. And I bet there's another room under this one."

"Great idea," I told Steve.

So we started digging. Since I was standing over the blue clay block in the middle of the room, I knew it probably meant something.

Maybe I'll find the treasure, I thought as I kept digging. *If I find the treasure, I'm going to use it to buy a year's supply of cake and video games... Maybe I can buy a new little brother too.*

All of a sudden we heard a *CLICK!* The floor collapsed again!

"AAAHHHHHHH!!!!"

THUD! THUD! THUD! THUD!

Oh man, that hurt.

I felt like somebody was sitting on me, so when I opened my eyes I wasn't surprised to find Steve, Piggy and Wesley all piled on top of me.

I guess it's good that they did, because I don't know if Steve could've survived that fall. Humans are real fragile, you know. On the other hand, Zombies are really tough. We can fall from a really high distance and be OK.

Especially little Zombies. One time Wesley fell out of my second floor bedroom window and he just bounced around like a rubber ball.

Actually, when I was little, Dad and I used to jump off the roof just for fun. Except one time

66

Dad landed on a rake, and it took Mom a few hours to get it out of him. Every time Dad turned around he would hit Mom on the back of the head. It was classic!

All the other guys were moaning and saying how tired they were. I don't know how they could be so tired after that fall, but they just fell asleep.

Funny, I was tired too. Maybe I should take a nap too.

It's really hard to write this journal entry being so tired. But I have to.

Who knows, if we never make it out of here, this may be my last words, ever...

Wednesday, I think...

I woke up to the taste of bacon in my mouth.

Urrrghhhblechhh!

Somehow, Piggy's foot ended up in my mouth! Yeecchhh!!!

Then Steve woke up.

"Oh my head," Steve said. "How long were we out?"

"I don't know," I said. "Maybe a few hours."

Then Piggy and Wesley woke up.

"I had the weirdest dream that a fish was sucking on my toes," Piggy said.

I didn't say anything about that.

"Where are we?" Steve said.

"Whoa," Piggy said looking around at all of the chests on the wall. "I think this is the treasure room."

"Treasure?!!" Steve said all excited.

"Yeah, but I bet they all have booby traps," I said, not quite as excited as everyone else.

We looked around, and the only thing that looked weird was a gray plate in the middle of the room, right next to my foot.

"What's this gray plate in the middle of the room?" I carefully backed away from it.

"It's a pressure plate," Steve said, "And I bet it's connected to a booby trap."

So everybody stepped really gently away from it.

Then we heard a creaking noise. We turned around and Wesley had opened one of the chests and was looking inside.

"Well, at least we know that chest isn't booby trapped," Steve said.

We looked and there was a book inside.

"We better not touch it," I said, "it's probably booby trapped."

I looked at the other guys to make sure they agreed with me, when I heard, "Shiny!"

Wesley had moved the book and there was a big fat diamond under it.

"Oooooohhhhh... Shiny!" Steve said, as his eyes grew really big.

Piggy picked up the book and started reading it. A minute later, he said, "Hey guys, I think this book can show us a way out of here."

"Really?" I went over to look at the book with Piggy.

"Yeah, it shows pictures of an underground minecart system that the Egyptian Zombies used to transport supplies."

"What's that?" I pointed to the picture of the floor collapsing under an Egyptian guy who was holding a big diamond.

"It just says the same warning as before: 'Beware, all who enter here. Only the noble will survive.'"

"Hey Steve, come check this out... Steve?"

"Oooooohhhhh… Shiny!" Steve said.

The picture suddenly made sense. "Oh no."

Steve picked up the diamond, and the floor collapsed under us again!

"AAAAAHHHHH!!!!!"

THUD! THUD! THUD! THUD!

Except this time, we all landed in a minecart.

The minecart was on a rail on a very steep hill. So when we landed, the impact made the minecart move and start going down the hill like a roller coaster.

"AAAAAHHHHH!!!!!"

We were going faster and faster through all kinds of underground tunnels and hills.

"WE'RE ALL GOING TO DIE, RUYEEKK!!!!" Piggy squealed.

72

Then I noticed that the walls were changing from sandy white to clay red.

"Hey! I think we're in the Mesa Biome!" I said.

But the guys didn't care. We were all just worried about how we were going to stop.

Then we saw it.

Ahead of us, we could see the end of the line. It was just one big, solid clay wall. We were going like a hundred miles an hour, so we were either going to go through it, or we were going to be splattered against it.

"EVERYBODY GET DOWN AND HOLD ON!!!" Steve said.

BOOOOOMMM!

We went right through the wall, and landed in a big cavern.

The minecart flipped over and we all crashed against the other wall.

I thought Steve was dead for sure, but when I looked over at him, Wesley and Piggy had grabbed onto him so tight that they had protected him from the impact.

I realized I grabbed onto him too, at least my body was still holding onto him. My head was looking at my body from the other side of the cave, so I knew I had issues.

Perfect time for another nap, I thought.

Thursday?

I woke up to my head swinging around.

"Don't worry, buddy," Steve said. "I'll put you back together."

So Steve put my head back on my body, and everything was right with the world.

Except when I looked down and saw my Zombie butt, I knew something wasn't right.

Steve, Piggy, and Wesley were laughing at me so I knew they did it on purpose.

"Guys, come on!" I said.

"Sorry, we thought we could use a good laugh right now," Steve said as he put my head on right.

Then far away in the cavern, we could see a light that was slowly fading.

"That must be the way out!" Steve said.

We picked up all of our stuff and headed toward the light.

When we got to the edge of the cave, we saw that the sun was going down. When it finally went down we went outside and looked around.

Everything was made of bright red clay.

"We made it to the Mesa Biome!" I said excitedly. "Now we just need to figure out how to get to the Grand Zombie Canyon."

"Yeah, except we don't know which way to go," Steve said.

We looked over the horizon and saw some smoke coming from down the hill. So we decided to walk over there to see if we can ask for directions.

When we got there, we found the strangest looking Zombie making some stew over a fire.

"Excuse me, sir," I said. "Can you help us find the Grand Zombie Canyon?"

All of a sudden he jumped up like something had bit him on the butt.

"Whoa! What you fellers trying to do, sneaking up on me like that?" he said.

"Sorry sir, we're just trying to find our way to the Grand Zombie Canyon."

"You're lost, are ye?" he said. "Well, I reckon it's a full two night's walk in that direction." He pointed toward the horizon.

"Two nights?!!"

"Yep, but you know, there's a town a few miles ahead, where yez can get a good night sleep and some food, for yer long journey."

"Yeah, that sounds good," Steve said. "So which way is it?"

"Oh, it's down the road, over the hill, through the mountains, around the creek, under the rock that looks like a big carrot, and up the path... Can't miss it."

"Thank you, Mr...?"

"Call me Prospector Joe," he said spitting. "Been prospecting this land for 30 years, searching for diamonds. This is my land, it is… SPIT!"

"Oh, Ok. Thanks Prospector Joe," I said as we walked toward the town.

There was something weird about that guy, I thought.

I just couldn't put my finger on it.

Thursday Late
I think...

"We've been walking around for hours," I said. "Where is this place?"

"Well, we went down the road, over the hill, through the mountains, around the creek, under the rock that looks like a big carrot, and up the path," Steve said. "I wonder if we missed something."

I was thinking, *we'd better find it fast because the sun will be rising soon.*

"There it is!" Piggy said

We looked down a steep cavern, and on the bottom we could see a small town.

"Oh man, I got a bad feeling about this," I said to Steve.

We got to the bottom of the cavern and walked into the town. Only problem was that the place was totally deserted. There were no mobs around: no Zombies, no Skeletons, no Creepers, no Slimes; not even an Enderman moving stuff around.

"This place gives me the creeps," Piggy said.

"What is this place?" I asked Steve.

Then we saw it, a wanted poster that looked like it'd been posted up years ago.

"Hey, isn't that...?"

"You mean the weird Zombie we met before?" Steve said, finishing my sentence.

"Why do I get the feeling that we're in trouble?" I said.

82

"Hey guys…" Piggy said, in a trembling voice, "Look."

We all looked up, and there was a gang of rough looking Zombies on Zombie horses, with prospector Joe leading the bunch. We turned around and there was another group behind us.

"Where do yer think yer going?" Prospector Joe called out in a smug voice.

"Uh… Mr. Prospector Joe sir… We were just going to our Zombie family reunion, he, he," I said.

"I know what you're up to. You're trying to get me diamonds, you is." He spat again. "Well, it ain't gonna happen… Get'em, boys!"

All of a sudden, the Zombies got off their horses and jumped at us.

83

Before they could grab us, Steve put Wesley down and yelled, "Run, Wesley, Run!"

Wesley ran around the gang of Zombies so fast they couldn't catch him. He bit them on the ankles and they started hopping around.

One thing about little Zombies is that they're really hard to catch.

We weren't so fast or so lucky.

"Run, Wesley, Run!!!" We all yelled as they put us in some sacks and took us to who knows where.

By now I'm not sure what day it is...

We travelled for a while. They wouldn't tell us where we were going. I heard us get on some minecarts so I know we went really far. I'm starting to think that not only will I miss the Zombie family reunion, I won't make it out of this alive!

Finally, we arrived somewhere that was really hot.

They carried us on their shoulders for a while and it got hotter and hotter.

I was really worried about little Wesley, though. *I hope he got away*, I thought. *Even though he's my pesky little brother, I wouldn't want anything to happen to him.*

Then they dumped us all on the ground:

THUD! THUD! THUD!

They took us out of the sacks and we were in a cave next to a pool full of lava.

"Let's just see if staying here fer a while will loosen your tongues up a bit," Prospector Joe said laughing. "Come on, boys, if they're not ready to talk when we get back, we'll just have to throw'em in. Heya, heya, heya!"

When they walked out, I saw the cave wasn't just a cave—it had bars to keep us in. Then they slammed the jail cell door of the cave and locked it behind them.

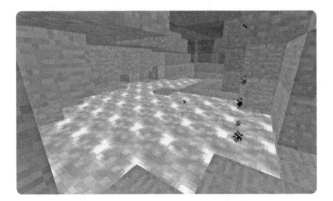

"Man, it's really hot down here," Steve said.

"You're not kidding," I said, "Zombies don't sweat, you know."

"It's not so bad. It kind of reminds me of home." Piggy shrugged, looking around.

"Well, we need to find a way out of here," Steve said. "What's the plan?"

"I don't know, Steve. I'm kind of feeling like it's hopeless," I said.

Then I started crying.

"You, OK, buddy?" Steve put his hand on my shoulder.

"Yeah, it's just that I'm really worried about Wesley, you know. He's all alone out there and who knows what they did to him. I know he's my little brother and he's a pest, but I'm really worried about him."

Then all of a sudden we heard, "Zumbie!"

We ran to the jail cell door.

"It's Wesley!!!"

"Wesley, great going, buddy," Steve said, "You got away from those guys."

I grabbed Wesley's hand and I said, "Wesley, I'm so glad you're OK. And I'm really sorry about all of those things I said about you. You're the best little brother anybody could ever have. But you have to go now, buddy. I don't know what's going to happen to us down here, and I want you to be safe, OK?" I said crying.

Wesley just looked at me with a big smile on his face and said, "Shiny!" as he held up the keys to the jail cell.

So, we took the keys and escaped.

But we could hear the gang of Zombies right behind us.

"They must know we escaped," Steve said. "Run!"

We ran into every cave we could find, but we didn't know which way to go.

Then we ran into a big cave in front of us, but it was a dead end.

All of a sudden, Prospector Joe and his thugs came in and cornered us.

"This is the end of the line for you boys," he said. "What do you think, Wilbur, should we feed them to the brain eating humans, heya, heya?"

"Yeah, Joe! I'm sure the pig is going to make a nice breakfast for those humans! Heya, heya, heya!"

Piggy got really scared when he heard that and started to cry, "Squeal, Squeal, Ruyeek… Not the humans, please not the humans!" And he curled up into a little ball on the floor.

All of a sudden, Steve stepped forward. He was madder than I had ever seen him before.

"You want to see some brain eating humans?!!!"

Then he wiped the green makeup off his face, and yelled, "YAARRRGGGHHHH!!!!!"

"He's a brain eating human!!!!" Prospector Joe yelled. His gang started screaming.

They all turned white and fell over each other trying to run away.

90

"YARRRGGGHHHH!!!!!" Steve kept yelling.

Prospector Joe and his goons ran away as fast as they could.

"That'll show them to mess with us again!" Steve said.

Then we looked over at Piggy and he was staring at Steve, still scared, in his little ball.

"Please don't eat my brains, Steve… Squeal, squeal, ruyeek," Piggy said.

"Don't worry, Piggy, I only eat regular Zombie brains," Steve said smiling.

"Whoa," Piggy said.

Steve looked at me, and said, "Just kidding."

So we made our way through the underground tunnels until we found a sign that said:

MINECARTS TO GRAND ZOMBIE CANYON THIS WAY

"Hey, guys, look!" I said. "This is the way to the Grand Zombie Canyon!"

We made it to the minecarts, but there weren't any left. I think the prospectors took them all running away from Steve.

But Piggy found an old broken down one without brakes.

"Will this work?" he asked.

"You bet it will," Steve said.

"Anything to get out of this place and see my Mom and Dad again," I said.

"Well, it doesn't have any brakes, but that never stopped us before," Steve said. "Hey, who's up for another minecart ride?"

"Les do id!" Wesley said.

So we all jumped into the minecart. Steve took a running start and jumped into the minecart to push us forward.

Well, hopefully we're on our way to Grand Zombie Canyon. Hopefully, I'll see Mom and Dad again. And hopefully we'll make it to our Zombie family reunion.

After everything else that's happened to us, nothing else could possibly be worse.

…Right?

Feels like Saturday...

Boy was I wrong!

The minecart ride was so long that all of us fell asleep.

We came to stop somewhere, and woke up to the sound of a chicken clucking.

I blinked and saw a chicken standing on my face.

"Hey can somebody get this chicken off me?" I said.

"Chicken!" Wesley said as he chased it around.

When we got out of the minecart, we saw that we were in another big underground cavern.

"I wonder where we are now?" I said, discouraged that we were still lost.

"Listen... Can you hear that?" Steve asked, tilting his head to hear better.

It sounded like music.

Then I realized where we were..."We must be right under the Grand Zombie Canyon!" I said. "That must be the music from the Zombie family reunion!"

"YEEAAAHHH!!!" we all yelled.

Then all of a sudden, we felt a big rumble. Then a bunch of big rocks crashed down.

"Look out!" Steve yelled, as rocks fell down from the cave ceiling. We ran for cover.

When it stopped, Steve said, "This place must be really unstable. Any loud sound can cause a cave-in."

95

So we quietly walked through the cave tunnels looking for a way out. Except for our clucking chicken. It wasn't that quiet.

I thought I saw a light coming from behind a pile of rocks in front of us, so I pointed it out to the guys.

When we started moving the rocks out of the way, we found a cave with a bright redstone torch in it.

After we moved enough rocks out of the way, we couldn't believe what we saw.

There was a skeleton in a uniform on the floor with a gold sword in one hand and a book in the other.

"Whoa, what's that?" Piggy asked.

"It looks like a soldier," Steve said. "I wonder what he's doing here."

"Hey, my Mom said that the last battle of the last Zombie Apocalypse was fought in the Grand Zombie Canyon," I said. "I wonder if he was a soldier from the war."

"But you said that Zombies don't die," Steve said, checking out the body. "This guy's been dead a long time."

Steve sat the soldier up to get a better look at him, and then we all saw it.

There was big crack and a hole in the skeleton's skull.

"Look." Steve pointed to some big rocks next to him. "He must have been hit on the head by some of those falling rocks."

"Yeah, my Dad said that the only thing that could kill a Zombie is a really hard blow to the head."

Piggy saw the gold sword and wanted to get it. But as he reached for it, he slipped and fell.

"SQUEAL!" he yelled as he fell down.

Suddenly, the rumbling started happening again. Except this time giant boulders started falling.

"IT'S A CAVE-IN!" Steve yelled, "EVERYBODY GET DOWN!"

Boulders and rocks started falling from all over the place. And then after a few minutes it stopped.

"Cough, cough… Is everybody OK?" Steve called out.

"Yeah, we're good," I said. Then I looked at the entrance to the cave and said, "Oh no!"

We all looked at the entrance, and it was totally blocked by giant boulders.

"Quick, try to help me move some of these," Steve said.

But no matter how hard we tried, they wouldn't budge.

"Oh man, I think we're stuck in here," Steve said.

Steve's words echoed through the cave, along with the music from the party that was going on up above.

We were so close, I thought.

Then something came over me and I yelled at the top of my voice, "HEEEELLLPPP!!!"

Then the rumbling started happening again, except this time the entire ceiling started slowly coming down. It stopped after dropping about a foot.

That's when I realized that we couldn't even call for help.

We were stuck.

This may be my last entry ever...

We were in the cave for hours. It actually felt like an entire day passed by.

We were tired, and we were hungry.

Steve kept looking at Wesley's chicken in weird ways, so I knew that the situation was affecting him too.

Piggy was passing the time by reading from the Zombie soldier's journal. He was really into it, reading page after page.

"Hey, what are you reading, Piggy?" I asked him.

"This book is amazing! It's the soldier's first-hand experience of the entire Zombie Apocalypse," Piggy said. "I'm actually reading his last entry. I'll read it to you..."

Private Sherman Zombie—234th Infantry

This May Be My Last Entry Ever…

We've been stuck in this cave for the past 103 days.

We can't call for help, because the cave is so unstable that even the slightest noise will cause a cave-in. Every day we have to avoid getting hit by rocks that randomly fall down on us.

My big brother Rhemus is trying to do his best to stay positive, but I can see in his eyes that he knows that our hope is lost.

All we have is our little redstone torch to give us a little light. And all I can do is pass the time writing about our experiences down here. But my pencil is going to run out soon.

Even though I may never feel the fresh night air on my face ever again, the one good thing is that my brother is right here with me.

I know we've had our troubles. Brothers always do. But I now realize that having a brother is the best gift any Zombie could ask for.

There's the rumbling sound again.

I hope I..."

We were quiet for a long moment.

"And that was the last entry," Piggy said.

"Did he say that his brother's name was Rhemus?" I asked Piggy.

"Yeah, why?"

"This must be my great, great, great, great, grandpa Rhemus' little brother," I said. "Which means that grandpa Rhemus found a way out of here, and we can too! Come on!"

All of a sudden, something came over me. I was so determined to find a way out that I didn't care about the falling rocks anymore. I was just trying to move rock after rock to see if we could make a hole big enough for us to get out.

The other guys got inspired and started moving rocks too.

"Hey, I feel fresh air!" Steve said as he created a small hole at the top of the pile of rocks.

"Can you get through there?" I asked Steve.

"Naw, it's too small for any of us," he said.

Then we all turned around and looked at Wesley.

Little Wesley just said, "Les do id!"

We moved fast to get Wesley and his new chicken through the hole.

"Follow the music, Wesley," I told him. "Find Mom and Dad. And find grandpa Rhemus. He knows how to find us."

As I said goodbye to him, the cave started rumbling again and the ceiling dropped another foot, covering the hole we made.

So now it's up to Wesley, I thought. Now it was up to my little brother who I called a pest most of his life. The little brother I got mad at a lot and bullied sometimes. The little brother that I used to be jealous of because Mom and Dad paid more attention to him than to me. The little brother that I wished had never been born.

My little brother Wesley…that I might not ever see again...

Wesley, if I don't make it out, and you find my journal, I just want to tell you that you are the best little brother that any Zombie could ever have.

And I love you with all my heart and I always will…

Monday

I woke up today to the rumbling sound of the cave.

I think that's going to be the last rumbling sound I will ever hear, I thought.

You see, the cave ceiling had almost totally collapsed so that it was an inch from my face.

Steve and Piggy were also trapped, but they were still OK. We just kept each other talking to pass the time.

All I was hoping for was that Wesley was OK, and that he found his way safely out of the cave.

Suddenly, we heard some voices.

"There it is!" I heard somebody say.

"Quick! Zeke, Billy Ray, Mabel, Otis, Roscoe, move that big boulder out from in front of the cave! But be careful, there could be another cave-in."

Then I heard a big boulder move as the cave started to rumble again.

"Mutant, put your back up against the ceiling," I heard.

UUURRRGGHHH!!!!

"Alright everybody, dig!"

I heard a bunch of digging noises and then I felt a hand feeling around my face.

"I got one!"

Then somebody grabbed me by the collar and dragged me out to the blinding light of somebody's torch.

"Zombie!" I heard voices that sounded like my Mom and Dad.

"Mom…Dad…Piggy and Steve are still…in there." I said, too weak to talk.

"Mutant, push up that ceiling!"

"UURRRGGHHHH!!"

Then I heard somebody say, "I smell bacon! I think I got another one!"

And they dragged Piggy out.

Then I heard somebody say, "I smell pickles! I think I got the last one!"

And they yanked Steve, covered in dust, out of the rubble.

"Is that everybody? Alright Mutant, let it go!"

"UUUURRRRGGGHHHH!!!!"

BOOOOMMMM!!!

"Everybody out, before the cavern falls down on us!!!"

All I remember after that is that I was on Dad's shoulders being carried out of the cave. Piggy, clutching the soldier's diary, was being carried by his Dad. And Mutant was carrying Steve.

Then everything went black…

Tuesday

When I woke up, I was in bed.

I looked around and it looked like I was in a hospital cave of some kind.

I looked out of the cave entrance and noticed that it was night out. I could hear music in the background so I knew that I was still at the Zombie family reunion.

As I looked over to the other beds, I could see my Mom giving water to Steve.

Steve! I thought, *Oh no! What if Mom finds out?*

Mom saw that I was awake and came over to my bed.

"How are you feeling, Zombie?" Mom asked.

"I'm OK," I said. But all I was thinking about was Mom finding out about Steve.

She saw me looking in Steve's direction and said, "Oh, don't worry about Zven. His secret is safe with us."

She didn't care? Wow, sometimes my mom can really surprise me.

"There's somebody here that was really worried about you," Mom said.

"Zumbie," Wesley said climbing on my bed.

"Wesley!" I gave him such a big hug that I think I hurt something.

Wesley looked at me and said, "I lub you too, Zumbie."

Then he took off riding on his new chicken.

When I finally got up, I saw that both Piggy and Steve were sleeping. By Piggy's bed was the soldier's diary from the cave. I picked it up because I knew what I had to do with it.

When I got out of the cave I saw hundreds of my relatives everywhere. I saw uncle Rufus and his whole family. I saw Piggy's parents. I saw my uncle Wither and the mess he was making everywhere. And, I even saw Mutant.

I never knew that Mutant was part of my family. But I always knew that Mutant and I had a special connection. All Zombies are related anyway, so I wasn't really surprised to see him there.

Dad came up to me, and a really old Zombie that was covered in medals hobbled alongside of him.

"Zombie, it's great to see you're feeling better," Dad said. "I have someone special I want to introduce to you."

"Zombie, this is grandpa Rhemus," Dad said.

"How are you, sir?" I asked.

"I'm fine," he said. "More importantly, how are you?"

"I'm feeling better," I said. Then I took the soldier's journal out of my pocket.

"Grandpa Rhemus, I think this belongs to you," I said.

His eye sockets grew really big as he looked at the journal.

"It's Sherman's journal," he said as his eye sockets started tearing up.

"You really loved your brother, didn't you?" I asked him.

"Sherman was the best little brother any Zombie could have," he said. "Thank you, Zombie, you don't know how much this means to me."

"Well, Zombie, are you ready for some cake?" Dad asked.

Boy was I ever!

Then all of a sudden, the music stopped and everybody got quiet.

They all stared in horror at the hospital cave. When I turned around, I saw that Steve had woken up and walked out of the hospital cave looking as human as he had ever been.

Oh man, now were in big trouble, I thought.

"IT'S A BRAIN EATING HUMAN!" somebody yelled.

All of a sudden everything went crazy.

But then, somebody yelled really loudly, "SIIIILLLLENCE!!!!"

A rickety old Zombie walked through the crowd toward Steve.

He came up to him and looked him over.

I could see on Steve's face that he thought he was dead for sure.

Then the rickety old man yelled, "HE'S OK!"

"Heerrraayyyy!!!! He's OK!!!!" Everybody yelled.

Then the music started again and everybody went back to their partying.

"Dad, what was that all about?" I asked him.

"Oh, didn't you know? Grandpa Methuselah used to be human before became a Zombie," Dad said. "He fell in love with Grandma Smelda Zombie about 900 years ago, and decided to switch sides. But he still has a soft spot for humans."

Then Steve, Piggy, Wesley and I, and the rest of the Zombie clan, just partied till daylight.

Wednesday

So this has been the best summer ever.

But unfortunately it has to come to an end.

School starts in a few weeks, and I'm actually looking forward to going back.

I'm looking forward to seeing my best friends Skelee, Slimey and Creepy again. And I'm really looking forward to seeing my ghoulfriend Sally.

I thought I was going to spend the whole summer playing video games and eating cake. But I wouldn't trade the summer I had for all of the video games or cake in the Overworld.

So, I'm going into eighth grade this year, which is really scary.

I think it means that I need to grow up.

But whatever is in store for me, and no matter how difficult it gets, the one thing I can count on are the love of my family and the love of my friends.

And, I can especially count on my best bud Steve.

So, get ready eighth grade, here I come!

Find out What Happens Next in...

Diary of a Minecraft Zombie Book 8
"Back To Scare School"

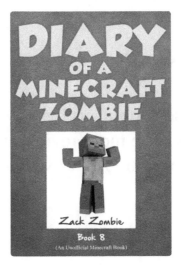

Get Your Copy and Join Zombie on More Exciting Adventures!

If you really liked this book, please tell a friend. I'm sure they will be happy you told them about it.

Leave Us a Review Too

Please support us by leaving a review. The more reviews we get the more books we will write!

Check Out All of Our Books in the Diary of a Minecraft Zombie Series

The Diary of a Minecraft Zombie Book 1
"A Scare of a Dare"

In the first book of this hilarious Minecraft adventure series, take a peek in the diary of an actual 12 year old Minecraft Zombie and all the trouble he gets into in middle school.

Get Your Copy Today!

The Diary of a Minecraft Zombie Book 2
"Bullies and Buddies"

This time Zombie is up against some of the meanest and scariest mob bullies at school. Will he be able to stop the mob bullies from terrorizing him and his friends, and make it back in one piece?

Jump into the Adventure and Find Out!

The Diary of a Minecraft Zombie Book 3
"When Nature Calls"

What does a Zombie do for Spring break?
Find out in this next installment of the exciting
and hilarious adventures of a 12 year old
Minecraft Zombie!

Get Your Copy Today!

The Diary of a Minecraft Zombie Book 4
"Zombie Swap"

12 Year Old Zombie and Steve
have Switched Bodies!
Find out what happens as 12 year old
Zombie has to pretend to be human and
Steve pretends to be a zombie.

Jump into this Zany Adventure Today!

The Diary of a Minecraft Zombie Book 5
"School Daze"

Summer Vacation is Almost Here and
12 Year Old Zombie Just Can't Wait!
Join Zombie on a Hilarious Adventure as
he tries to make it through the last few
weeks before Summer Break.

Jump into the
Adventure Today!

The Diary of a Minecraft Zombie Book 6
"Zombie Goes To Camp"

Join 12 year old Zombie, as he faces his biggest fears, and tries to survive the next 3 weeks at Creepaway Camp.
Will he make it back in one piece?

Jump into His Crazy Summer Adventure and Find Out!

The Diary of a Minecraft Zombie Book 7
"Zombie Family Reunion"

Join Zombie and his family on their crazy
adventure as they face multiple challenges
trying to get to their 100th Year
Zombie Family Reunion.
Will Zombie even make it?

Get Your Copy Today
and Find Out!

The Diary of a Minecraft Zombie Book 8
"Back to Scare School"

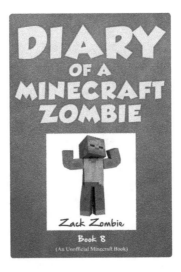

Zombie finally made it through 7th grade...
And he even made it through one really crazy
summer! But will Zombie be able to survive
through the first weeks of being an 8th grader
in Mob Scare School?

Find Out in His Latest
Adventure Today!

The Diary of a Minecraft Zombie Book 9
"Zombie's Birthday Apocalypse"

It's Halloween and it's Zombie's Birthday!
But there's a Zombie Apocalypse happening that
may totally ruin his Birthday party.Will Zombie
and his friends be able to stop the Zombie
Apocalypse so that they can finally enjoy some
cake and cookies at Zombie's Birthday Bash?

Jump into the Adventure
and Find Out!

The Diary of a Minecraft Zombie Book 10
"One Bad Apple"

There's a new kid at Zombie's middle
school and everyone thinks he is so cool.
But the more Zombie hangs out with him, the
more trouble he gets into. Is this new Mob kid
as cool as everyone thinks he is, or is he really a
Minecraft Wolf in Sheep's clothing?

Jump Into this Zany Minecraft Adventure and Find Out!